Raggedy Ann's
Tea Party Book

Simon & Schuster Books for Young Readers
An imprint of Simon & Schuster Children's Publishing Division
1230 Avenue of the Americas, New York, New York 10020

SIMON & SCHUSTER BOOKS FOR YOUNG READERS is a trademark of Simon & Schuster.
Book design by Lee Wade
The text for this book is set in Venetian.
The illustrations are rendered in watercolor.
Printed in Hong Kong
First Edition
10 9 8 7 6 5 4 3 2
Library of Congress Cataloging-in-Publication Data
Silbaugh, Elizabeth.
Raggedy Ann's tea party book / by Elizabeth Silbaugh ; illustrated by Laura Filippucci. — 1st ed.
       p.   cm.
Summary: Raggedy Ann shows the reader how to have a tea party—from sending out invitations
and preparing refreshments to planning games and setting the table.
ISBN 0-689-81855-6
1. Afternoon teas—Juvenile literature. 2. Children's parties—Juvenile literature. 3. Cookery—Juvenile literature.
[1. Afternoon teas. 2. Parties. 3. Cookery.] I. Filippucci, Laura, ill. II. Title.
TX736.S55 1999 641.5'3—dc21
98-17548
CIP AC

Raggedy Ann's
Tea Party Book

By Elizabeth Silbaugh

Illustrated by Laura Francesca Filippucci

Simon & Schuster Books for Young Readers

Raggedy Ann loves tea parties!

She learned about them from Marcella, the little girl who rescued her from the attic. Now Raggedy Ann has lots of tea parties and invites all the dolls from Marcella's room.

In this book you'll see how easy and fun it is to have your own tea party. Raggedy Ann will show you how!

Getting ready for a tea party can take some work, but it is worth it. Once the work is done, you'll be chatting with your friends as you sip tea and eat delicious little cakes and cookies.

The first thing to do is to decide on a place and time for your tea party. Will it be inside or outside? In the morning or in the afternoon? You'll also need to figure out how many guests you can invite. Do you have enough chairs for everyone? If not, maybe you can sit on the floor around a pretty blanket or table-cloth.

Next, think about which friends to invite. Maybe this tea party is just for you and your dolls. Or maybe you will ask a few friends to come along. Try not to hurt anyone's feelings by leaving someone out, but remember that it's nice to keep your party small and cozy. That way it'll be easier to prepare, and you can be sure you'll get to talk to everyone at the party.

Now it's time to send out the invitations. Making invitations is lots of fun, and your guests will be delighted to receive them!

With just a few simple supplies, you can make your own special invitations. This is what you'll need:

Construction paper or another pretty kind of paper

Envelopes

Ribbon, lace, or glitter for decorating the edges of your invitations

Glue

Crayons, markers, or paint

Scissors

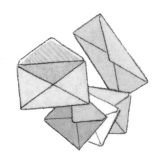

To make the invitations, cut the paper to any size and shape you like (so long as they fit into your envelopes!). You can make folded invitations with the party information inside the card, or simple invitations with all the information on the front.

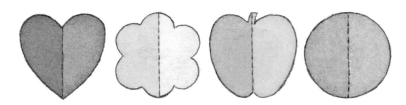

Don't forget to write when and where your party will take place. You can also add the letters "R.S.V.P." and your name and phone number. R.S.V.P. stands for *Respondez s'il vous plait,* which is French for "Respond, please," or "Let me know if you can come."

Last but not least, decorate your invitations! Cut the ribbon or lace to fit around the edges, or glue them onto the front. How about painting or drawing some designs or cutting out some red paper hearts? If you like, you can even add a small decoration to each envelope.

Next you'll need to decide what to serve at your tea party.
Here are some suggestions:

 scones and crumpets

cakes and cookies

 tarts

gingerbread

tea and lemonade

finger sandwiches

Ask an adult to help you come up with even more ideas for little treats you can make or buy for your party.

Remember: keep it simple! It's nice to have a few different things for your guests to nibble on, but don't try to prepare too much. The idea is to have *fun* getting ready for your party. If you'd like to try making your own treats, turn to page 24 for some of Raggedy Ann's favorite recipes.

The next step is to make a shopping list. Raggedy Ann and Marcella check their cupboards at home first to see if they already have some of the things they need.

Try to do your shopping or baking early so that you'll be ready to greet your guests when they arrive!

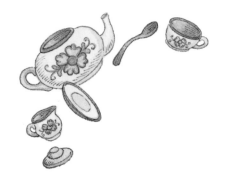

After you've finished shopping, it's time to prepare the food and get the table ready. A tablecloth—either plain or fancy—will make the room look festive. Bring extra chairs to the table if you need to.

Raggedy Ann asks the other dolls to help her. They put on some cheery music and dance as they go!

Setting the table is one of Raggedy Ann's very favorite parts of getting ready for a tea party. She loves to make the table look as pretty as she can. She shines up the cups and saucers and silverware and sometimes even makes place cards and folds the napkins in a special way.

Raggedy Ann also likes to add extra touches like flowers or a dish of strawberries, dried apricots, or chocolates.

After your work at the table is done, you have a little time to rest. You might also decide to dress up a bit for the party.

Marcella helps Raggedy Ann work the snarls out of her red-yarn hair. After washing her hands and face and putting on her prettiest pinafore, all that's left is to wait for the guests. This is the exciting part!

When your friends arrive, welcome them inside. Raggedy Ann leads each person to the table, making sure to introduce anyone who doesn't know the others.

Offer tea and lemonade to your guests and ask everyone to help themselves to cookies, cakes, and sandwiches. A tea party is the perfect time to use your best manners, so don't forget to say "please" and "thank you"! Some people practice being very formal and stick out their pinkie fingers when they hold their teacups. Can you do this? Take tiny sips of your tea, and remember to keep your mouth closed while chewing food.

Raggedy Ann says that the most important thing
about a tea party is that everyone has a good time.
Make sure to include all of your guests in the party
conversation and cheer.

Games make a tea party even more fun. Here are three of Raggedy Ann's favorites:

MEMORY TRAY

Gather ten or twenty small objects and put them on a tray. Cover the tray with a tea towel.

When you are ready to begin playing, set the tray in the middle of the table. Explain that you will allow two minutes for everyone to take a good look at the tray. Set a timer and remove the tea towel. When the two minutes are over, move the tray out of sight.

One by one, ask the guests to name one object they remember seeing on the tray. Go around the table, so that each person takes a turn. Ask a grown-up to make a list of the items you and your guests name, and see if you can remember everything that was on the tray!

FIDDLY DIDDLY

Fiddly diddly diddly dee,
I see something you can't see,
And the color of it is...

In this game, one person secretly thinks of something in the room and recites this rhyme, telling everyone what color the item is but saying nothing more about it. The first person to guess what the object is gets to choose the next object, and the game begins again.

TELEPHONE

To begin this game, ask someone to think of a message and whisper it to his or her neighbor at the table. That neighbor then whispers it to the next person, and so on, until the message gets all the way around the table. Try to repeat exactly what you hear. The last person to get the message says it out loud. Then the first person reveals what the original message was.

How well did the whisper-telephone work?

When all the games have been played and all the treats are gone, everyone agrees that this has been a perfectly wonderful tea party.

Raggedy Ann says "good-bye" to her last guest, and it is time to clean up. The dolls put on their music again and make it fun!

Later that night Raggedy Ann snuggles in bed, already thinking about her next tea party. Maybe she will have a simpler one this time, with some nice bread and jam from the cupboards. If it's a sunny day, maybe it can be a tea party picnic. Or maybe... Raggedy Ann drifts into sweet dreams of all kinds of marvelous tea parties.

What will your tea party be like?

Tea Party Recipes

Always ask an adult to help you make your goodies.

EASY CHOCOLATE CAKES

Preheat the oven to 350° so it will be nice and hot when you put the cakes in to bake. Carefully measure the following ingredients into a big bowl:

3 cups flour	2 teaspoons baking soda
2 cups sugar	1 teaspoon salt
2/3 cup cocoa powder	

With a big spoon, stir the mixture. Once it is all an even light brown color, add:

2 cups water	2/3 cup vegetable oil
2 teaspoons vanilla	2 teaspoons vinegar

Use your spoon to mix these wet ingredients into the dry ones. Keep stirring until most of the lumps are gone.

Now you are ready to spoon or pour the batter into ungreased cupcake pans. Leave some room for the cakes to rise during baking. There should be enough batter for about 18 cupcakes. (You can also use two 9-inch cake pans or one 9x13-inch rectangular pan—or even a heart-shaped pan, if you have one.)

Put the pans in the oven and set a timer for 20-25 minutes. When the bell rings, see whether the cakes are done by poking a toothpick into the middle of one of them. Is there any gloppy batter sticking to it? If there is, keep baking the cakes and testing every 5 minutes until a toothpick comes out clean.

When the cakes are done, let them cool for about 20 minutes before taking them out of the pans. One easy and pretty way to decorate these cakes is to sift powdered sugar onto each one through a heart-shaped stencil. Or you can frost the cakes with icing and sprinkle red hots or red sugar on top.

CREAMY PINK AND WHITE ICING

In a medium-size bowl, stir together:
  2 cups powdered sugar
  Pinch of salt

When they are well mixed, add:
  1 teaspoon vanilla
  1/2 cup cream

Beat the mixture with an electric beater until the icing is soft and creamy, just right for spreading on cakes.

Leave half of the icing in the bowl. This will be your white icing. With a spoon or rubber spatula, put the other half of the icing into a separate bowl. To make the icing pink, add two drops of red food coloring and stir with a spoon. If you need to, add another drop or two of food coloring until you get a pretty pink shade.

TINY SANDWICHES

Some people call these "finger sandwiches"—maybe because they can be shaped like fingers, or maybe because you can pick them up between your thumb and one finger.

To make these very delicate and elegant sandwiches, start with:

Very thinly sliced bread (either white bread or whole wheat bread, or both)
Cream cheese or butter

First, ask an adult to trim the crusts off several pieces of bread, using a sharp knife.

Then, spread each slice of bread with cream cheese or butter. Cream cheese and butter are hard to spread when they are very cold, so take them out of the refrigerator about an hour before you are going to make the sandwiches.

With an adult's help, make simple fillings for the sandwiches. You will use only one filling in each sandwich. Here are a few filling ideas:

very thin slices of ham, tomato, or hard-boiled egg

raspberry jam, ginger preserve, or orange marmalade

tuna fish

very thin slices of cheese with chutney on top

very thin slices of strawberries or bananas

very thin slices of cucumber

a few feathery stems of fresh dill

watercress leaves

Make a thin layer of one of the fillings on a piece of bread. Put another piece of bread on top. If you like, you can make a triple-decker sandwich by spreading the top slice with more cream cheese or butter, putting another layer of filling on top, and then adding another piece of bread. Put your sandwiches on a plate in the refrigerator for about an hour. This will make them easier to cut into fancy triangles, squares, or strips.

RAGGEDY ANN'S CANDY-HEART COOKIES

Carefully measure these ingredients into a large bowl:

2 sticks of butter   **I egg**

3/4 cup sugar   **I teaspoon vanilla**

I 3-ounce package of cream cheese

Using an electric beater, mix everything together on medium speed for 3-4 minutes. This will be easier if you use butter or cream cheese that has been out of the refrigerator for an hour.

Next, add:

3 cups flour

Beat in the flour until it is completely mixed in. This should take I-2 minutes on low speed. Wrap the ball of dough in wax paper and put it in the refrigerator for at least 2 hours or even overnight. Chilling the dough makes it easier to roll out and cut.

When the dough is cold enough, heat the oven to 325°.

Use a rolling pin to flatten the dough to about 1/4-inch thick. Cut out heart shapes using a knife or cookie cutter. If you like, sprinkle some or all of the hearts with red sugar.

Place the hearts on a cookie sheet and bake them for 7-9 minutes.

You can also use your dough to make the "baby teeny, weeny cookies" that Marcella and her dolls love so much—just cut the dough into tiny circles and bake them for 5 minutes.

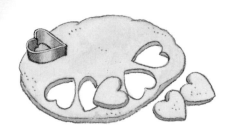

Uncle Clem's Super-Simple Scotch Shortbread

This does not take very many ingredients, and it is as tasty as can be!

Preheat the oven to 325°. Using a fork or an electric beater and a medium-size bowl, mash:

2 sticks of butter

This will be easier if the butter has been out of the refrigerator for about an hour. Keep beating the butter until it gets creamy.

In another medium-size bowl, stir together the following ingredients:

2 cups flour
1/2 cup powdered sugar
1/4 teaspoon salt

Pour this mixture into the bowl with the butter in it, and stir everything together until it turns into a smooth dough. With your fingers, press this dough into an ungreased square pan, 9x9 inches. Prick it with a fork about twenty times.

Put the pan in the oven and bake it for 25-30 minutes. Cut the shortbread into squares while it is still warm.

MARCELLA'S LEMONADE

It's nice to offer lemonade in case someone doesn't want tea.

This recipe makes enough for four guests. Start with:

3 lemons

Cut them in half with a knife and squeeze them with a lemon squeezer. Put the lemon juice in a pitcher and add:

1/2 cup sugar

Stir the mixture until the sugar dissolves. Be patient; this may take several minutes.

Next, add:

4 cups cold water

Plenty of ice cubes or crushed ice

Taste the lemonade to see if it needs more water, sugar, or lemon juice. Sometimes Marcella puts a spoonful of grape jelly in each glass to give it a lovely lavender color! If you like, you can try this too.

Walt Disney's
Snow White
and the White
Seven Dwarfs

ADAPTED FROM THE FILM BY
Jim Razzi

ILLUSTRATED BY
Fernando Guell and Fred Marvin

Disney
PRESS

NEW YORK

Text and illustrations © 1993 by Disney Press.
All rights reserved.
No part of this book may be used or reproduced in any manner whatsoever
without written permission from the publisher.
Printed and bound in the United States of America.
For information address Disney Press,
114 Fifth Avenue, New York, New York 10011.
1   3   5   7   9   10   8   6   4   2
Library of Congress Catalog Card Number: 92-53430
ISBN 1-56282-362-0/1-56282-363-9 (lib. bdg.)

Walt Disney's
Snow White
and the White
Seven Dwarfs

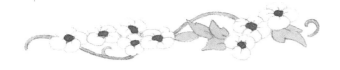

CHAPTER ONE

n a little kingdom graced with rolling hills, sparkling rivers, and bountiful forests, there once lived a lovely young princess named Snow White. Snow White was not only kind but beautiful as well. Her hair was the deepest ebony, her complexion the purest ivory.

Snow White's father, the king, was dead, and so she lived in the palace with her stepmother, the queen. And although the queen was also very beautiful, her beauty was only skin deep. Inside she was cold and heartless and as evil as an ugly old witch.

The queen was very jealous of Snow White's beauty. So much so that she forced the little princess to dress in tattered rags and made her work long hours as a scullery maid.

The queen thought that, disguised in this way, Snow White's beauty could never rival her own. Still, that wasn't enough to satisfy her vanity.

In a dark and foreboding part of the castle, the queen kept a magic mirror. And every day she would stand before the ornate mirror and chant, "Magic mirror on the wall, who is the fairest of them all?"

And every day, the surface of the mirror would swirl like a dark whirlpool, and a grim face would appear, as if rising from the depths.

"*You* are the fairest one of all," the face would answer.

The queen would smile and nod and be content.

As time went on, however, Snow White's beauty became more and more apparent in spite of the queen's efforts to hide it. So it was that on one bright and sunny day, when the queen asked the mirror her usual question, it replied in its deep, somber voice:

> *Famed is thy beauty, Majesty,*
> *but hold—a lovely maid I see—*
> *rags cannot hide her gentle grace.*
> *Alas, she is more fair than thee.*

The queen stiffened in shocked surprise. Then she lowered her eyebrows and said, "Alas for *her.* Reveal her name."

And the face in the mirror answered:

> *Lips red as a rose, hair black as ebony,*
> *skin white as snow . . .*

"Snow White!" the queen hissed.

At the very moment the queen was consulting her magic mirror, Snow White was busy scrubbing the stone steps of the courtyard below. The work was hard, but Snow White performed the task in good spirits. And now she sang prettily as a flock of white doves fluttered around her, cooing and bobbing.

When she turned to draw water from a nearby well, Snow White peered down at her reflection and was quite startled to see another face next to hers.

"Oh!" she cried. Looking up, she saw a handsome man in the fine dress of a prince standing right beside her.

"Oh!" she cried again, backing away.

"Did I frighten you? I didn't mean to," the prince said with concern. "It's just that I heard such a lovely song as I was riding by."

Snow White was so flustered she couldn't speak. Finally, she bolted toward the castle door, scattering the doves in her wake.

"Wait! Please don't go," cried the prince. "I'd like to talk to you some more." But Snow White was already running up the castle's winding stone steps to a small balcony that overlooked the courtyard. When she reached the balcony, she peeked past the heavy curtains and looked down.

The prince was still there, gazing up at the castle. He looked so handsome and seemed so kind that Snow White felt drawn to him.

Timidly at first and then more boldly, she stepped closer to the balcony's edge.

When the prince saw her, he couldn't help but smile. She was the most beautiful girl he had ever seen.

"Please come back," he urged. "I must get to know you."

Snow White smiled, too, but still did not move from the balcony.

As the prince continued to entreat her to return, a dove flew up onto Snow White's hand. On impulse, she kissed the

dove and bade it fly down to the young man below. The dove gently fluttered down to the prince and kissed him in return. The prince blushed and cried, "I shall never forget you!"

And with that, Snow White withdrew into the dark castle.

Unknown to either Snow White or the prince, the queen had been watching this tender scene, which filled her with even more anger and jealousy.

Now the ruler nodded as if she had made up her mind to carry out an evil plan. And in fact, she had. She called her chief huntsman to her throne.

When the huntsman arrived, the queen commanded him in a firm voice, "Take Snow White far into the forest. Find some secluded glade where she can pick wildflowers."

"Yes, Your Majesty," answered the huntsman.

"And there, my faithful huntsman, you will *kill* her!"

Although the huntsman was a hardened man, he gasped and stared up at his queen.

"But Your Majesty," he cried, "the little princess!"

"Silence!" snapped the queen. "You know the penalty if you fail."

The huntsman bowed his head.

"Yes, Your Majesty," he said solemnly.

Then the queen paused and held out an ornate red box. Its clasp was formed by a jeweled dagger piercing a golden heart.

"But to make doubly sure you do not fail," the queen continued, "bring back her *heart* in this."

The huntsman took the box and slowly nodded his head.

now White was soon wandering cheerfully through a lush green meadow, with the huntsman following close behind. She had been told that the queen wanted some wildflowers for her table, and she was glad of the chance to go out into the surrounding countryside.

She was reaching to pick from a cluster of bright daisies when she spied a baby bird on the ground beside a large rock. "Why, hello there," Snow White said.

The tiny creature shook its blue speckled wings and chirped a hello in response. Snow White bent down to pick up the bird and suddenly noticed a large, dark shadow creeping up the rock. She whirled around in fright and then cringed in terror as she saw the huntsman looming over her, a sharp knife in his hand. She pressed herself against the rock and put her hands up to shield her face.

The huntsman came at her grimly, his knife poised to strike. But at the last moment, his hand shook and his face fell in dismay.

"I can't do it," he cried as he dropped to his knees. "Forgive me. I beg of Your Highness, forgive me."

"Why . . . why . . . I don't understand," stammered the frightened princess.

"She's mad, jealous of you," the huntsman said. "She'll stop at nothing."

Snow White stared at the huntsman for a moment in shock and confusion. "But who?" she gasped.

"The queen!" answered the huntsman.

"The queen?" echoed Snow White, her face growing pale.

"Yes," said the huntsman. "Now quick, child. Run. Run away and hide!"

"But . . . where shall I go?" asked Snow White in a trembling voice.

"Into the woods—anywhere," said the huntsman, gesturing wildly at the thick forest just beyond the meadow. "Now go! Run and don't come back."

Without another word, Snow White whirled and fled into the dark forest. She could hear the huntsman urging her on as she stumbled blindly through dense trees and brush. And as she ran, the things in the forest took on shapes and forms she had never before imagined. The branches of trees sprang to life around her, their clawlike hands reaching out to grab her. Rocks became hunched wild animals ready to rear up at a moment's notice.

Snow White ran across a hilly bog, and all at once the spongy ground gave way underneath her and she fell into a dark pool full of half-rotted logs. As she frantically struggled to free herself from the murky waters, the floating logs were

transformed into terrifying crocodiles, snapping at her with wide jaws.

She finally stumbled out of the pool and ran again, deeper and deeper into the forest until she saw her path blocked by an enormous black tree. Its gnarled trunk showed a grotesque and frightening face, and its thick branches reached out as if to grab and crush her. Snow White screamed and stumbled into a nearby clearing. There she fell to the mossy earth, sobbing in terror until she was so exhausted that she fell fast asleep where she lay.

CHAPTER THREE

The next morning, as the rays of the rising sun streamed down into the woods, curious eyes peeked out from the surrounding trees and bushes and stared at the sleeping girl.

Three fawns bobbed their heads and then cautiously picked their way forward. They were joined by a group of chattering chipmunks and bushy-tailed squirrels zigzagging their way across the clearing. A rabbit family hopped out of its hiding place behind an old tree, followed by two black-eyed raccoons and a small flock of quail.

As a half dozen bluebirds fluttered down from the trees to join the other animals, one frisky little rabbit, bolder than the rest, hopped right up to Snow White. With a twitching pink nose it sniffed her hair. The princess stirred and raised her head. "Oh!" she cried.

The rabbit seemed as startled as Snow White, and it bounded away while the other creatures also scurried for cover.

Snow White looked around and said, "Please don't run away. I won't hurt you."

As if they understood her, the forest animals reappeared. Snow White smiled at them.

"I'm awfully sorry," she continued. "I didn't mean to frighten you all. But you don't know what I've been through!"

The gentle creatures now came out and surrounded her. A baby bluebird perched on Snow White's hand, and she was heartened by its trust.

"I really feel quite happy now," she said. "I'm sure I'll get along somehow."

The animals all nodded in agreement.

"But I do need a place to sleep," Snow White said. "Maybe you know where I can stay?" she asked the animals kindly.

A group of bluebirds chirped and twittered in response.

"You do?" Snow White cried as she rose to her feet. "Will you take me there?"

In answer, the birds took Snow White's cape with their small beaks and urged her to follow them. Soon a small parade of animals was following Snow White and the birds as they made their way through the tangled woods.

The birds led Snow White to a snug little house nestled deep in the forest.

As soon as she saw the cottage, Snow White's spirits rose. It was a tiny house with white walls and a brown thatched roof. A small wooden bench stood outside as if to welcome a weary traveler.

"Oh, it's adorable," Snow White murmured. "Just like a dollhouse. I like it here already," she said as she inspected the house from close up.

Snow White went to a window and wiped a clear circle in the grimy glass. "It's so dark inside," she said. "I don't think there's anyone home."

Nevertheless, she went back to the doorway, which was framed by leafy vines on either side, and politely knocked on the thick wooden door. No one answered.

She turned to the animals. "I guess there's no one home," she said.

She knocked again and waited, but there was no answer.

Then she noticed that the door had opened a crack. With brisk steps she entered the tiny house and called, "Hello! May I come in?"

No one answered.

Snow White ventured further into the house. And when she did, she stared around in wonder. Everything was so *small*!

"What a cute little chair!" she exclaimed.

Then she saw there were *seven* little chairs.

"Why, there must be seven little children living here," Snow White said to her animal friends.

And as she looked around, she also realized that the whole cottage was full of dust and dirt. The sink was filled with unwashed dishes, there were dirty clothes everywhere, and the fireplace looked as if it hadn't been swept out in years!

"Why, they've never swept this room," Snow White said. "You'd think their mother would . . ."

Then she paused as a thought occurred to her.

"Maybe they have no mother," she said.

The animals nodded their heads in sad agreement.

"Then they're orphans," Snow White said. "That's too bad."

She gazed around at the untidy little house for a long moment, then suddenly announced, "I know what we'll do!"

The animals all waited expectantly for Snow White to continue.

"We'll clean up and surprise them!" Snow White clapped her hands in satisfaction.

"Then when they see how helpful I can be, maybe they'll let me stay," she said.

Again the animals nodded as if they understood Snow White's intentions.

"Well, let's not just all stand here," she said with a good-natured laugh. "Let's get busy!"

And in no time at all they did.

The squirrels scurried cheerfully around the cottage, sweeping the floor and dusting off the furniture with their bushy tails.

The raccoons helped Snow White wash the clothes by rubbing the garments together between their paws to get them sparkling clean.

The birds eagerly flew up to every nook and cranny in the ceiling, pulling down cobwebs and balls of dust with their strong beaks.

The deer and the rabbits pushed and pulled tables and chairs into their proper places.

Even the tiny chipmunks gladly helped, carrying dirty

cups, dishes, and silverware in their paws and mouths and depositing them in a wooden sink to be washed.

With everyone doing their share, the work went smoothly throughout the afternoon as the sun slowly lowered to the west.

While all this was going on, the people who lived in the cottage were in the hills not far away, digging for jewels in a deep, dark mine. There were seven men in all, and they were dwarfs. And in spite of their different personalities, the dwarfs got along quite well together and worked side by side in perfect harmony. As they swung their picks and shovels, they sang a work song that echoed back to them throughout the caverns and tunnels of the mine.

Just as they started to sing another chorus, a clock in the mine struck five. One of the dwarfs looked up and cried, "Heigh-ho!" The others quickly collected their tools and marched out of the mine in single file. They traveled along a well-worn path that wound through woods and over rocky hills and small ravines. And all the while, they whistled and sang, content to be heading home after a good day's work.

Back at the cottage, Snow White and the animals looked around with pride at the sparkling-clean room. "Now let's see what's upstairs," she said.

Snow White led the way up the small wooden steps as the animals followed behind. She saw that there was a bedroom with seven little beds in it. On each wooden bed board, a name

was carved. Snow White looked at each one in turn.

"What funny names for children," she said. "Doc, Happy, Sneezy, Dopey . . ."

Snow White laughed as she continued reading, "Grumpy, Bashful, Sleepy . . ."

Just then she yawned.

"I'm a little sleepy myself," she murmured.

Snow White lay across three of the little beds and sighed. The animals gently pulled a sheet up to cover her and then, one by one, found cozy spots of their own. Snow White's eyes closed, and soon she and the forest creatures were fast asleep.

CHAPTER FOUR

s Snow White and her friends slept in the little cottage, the low sound of singing echoed through the forest. It woke the animals instantly. With tails twitching and noses quivering, they listened as the singing grew louder. It was the dwarfs making their way home from work!

With startled leaps and bounds, the deer, squirrels, rabbits, and chipmunks scampered out of the house and back into the woods, leaving Snow White still sleeping peacefully on the tiny beds.

As the dwarfs approached the house, Doc pointed and said, "Look! Our house—the lit's light—I mean, the light's lit!"

The dwarfs immediately took cover behind a grove of thick pines.

"Jiminy crickets!" they all cried at once.

"Door's open, chimney's smoking," said Doc. "Something's in there!"

"It . . . it may be a ghost," stammered Happy.

"Or a goblin," whispered Bashful.

"It might be a—*a-achoo*—dragon," said Sneezy, his nose tickled by the scent of the pines.

The other dwarfs glared at him and motioned him to be quiet.

Grumpy scowled and said, "Mark my words, there's trouble a-brewing. Felt it coming all day. My corns hurt."

The dwarfs all looked at each other in concern.

"What'll we do?" asked Sleepy. "I'm too sleepy to think."

"Let's sneak up on it," Happy exclaimed.

"Yes! Huh?" Doc answered, suddenly aware of what Happy was proposing. Then he stood up straighter and addressed the others. "We'll squeak up—uh, I mean, sneak up on it. Come on, hen—uh, men. Follow me!"

The dwarfs slowly and cautiously crept up to the house, one behind the other. When they got to the door, they filed in, quiet as mice, with Dopey in the rear. They were so close to each other they looked glued together. Suddenly Dopey slammed the door shut.

The dwarfs screamed and huddled against each other, expecting the worst. When they realized it was just Dopey, they put their fingers to their lips and said, *"Shhhh!"*

Dopey nodded. Then he turned to the door, put his finger to his lips, and repeated, *"Shhhh."*

As the dwarfs crept through the house, they noticed that things didn't seem quite the same as they had left them that morning.

"Look. The floor's been swept," said Doc.

Grumpy rubbed a finger along the top of a chair.

"Huh. Chair's been dusted," he said in disgust.

"And our window's been washed," cried Happy as he looked out at the forest beyond.

"Why, the whole place is clean," Doc finally announced.

"There's dirty work afoot!" growled Grumpy.

Just then Happy spied their big black kettle bubbling in the fireplace and sniffed.

"Something's cookin'," he said. "And it smells good!"

Happy grabbed a spoon and was about to dip it into the kettle when Grumpy snatched it away and yelled, "Don't touch it, ya fool, it might be poison!"

Glancing nervously around the room, the dwarfs felt sure that some sort of unknown and terrible creature had invaded their home.

CHAPTER FIVE

hile the dwarfs were creeping about below, some birds were hiding in the rafters above. Nodding and winking at each other, they knew who the unexpected visitor was. Suddenly they tapped their beaks against the rafters, and the dwarfs huddled together fearfully.

"Hear that?" whispered Grumpy. "Whatever it is, it's in this room, right now!"

The birds couldn't help twittering to themselves in mischievous delight. Suddenly they let out a high-pitched shriek, and the dwarfs tumbled all over themselves in panic and fright.

When they finally settled down once more, Doc pointed upstairs.

"It's . . . it's up there," he said in a low voice.

"Yeah, in the bedroom," agreed Bashful.

Doc nodded solemnly.

"One of us has got to go down and chase it up—uh, I mean, go up and chase it down," he said.

The dwarfs all nodded in agreement. Dopey nodded eagerly—even after everyone else had stopped. Finally, he noticed that the other dwarfs were all staring in his direction. He turned to look behind him, but there was no one there. They were staring at *him*. They wanted him to lead the way!

Dopey tried to run, but the dwarfs grabbed him. Doc handed him a candle.

"H-here, take it," said Doc, shaking. "D-don't be nervous."

The dwarfs pushed Dopey ahead of them, up the stairs.

"Don't be afraid," said Doc. "We're right behind you."

"Yeah, right behind you," echoed the others from a good distance.

Dopey took a deep gulp, climbed the darkened stairs to the bedroom, and slowly opened the door. A long, low moan emanated from the darkness, and in the flickering light of the candle, Dopey saw something moving underneath the sheets across three of the beds.

Suddenly the candle went out, and with a yelp, Dopey burst out of the bedroom and started to pound down the dark stairs.

"It's the creature!" the other dwarfs cried as they proceeded to fall all over each other, trying to get out of the way. They yelled and screamed and ran out of the cottage, slamming the door behind them. Once outside the house, they hid behind the pine trees and waited.

Meanwhile, Dopey thought the creature was right behind *him,* and in his frantic haste to escape he crashed into a cupboard, causing pots and pans to come tumbling out. One large soup pot fell over his head, and as he blindly stumbled about, he jammed one foot into another, smaller pot. Dizzily turning

this way and that, he finally groped his way out of the cottage and headed toward the other dwarfs.

"Here it comes!" yelled Happy as he saw the strange figure with the metal head clanking and clumping toward them.

"Now's our only chance, men!" said Doc. "We mustn't be spared—er, I mean, scared."

The dwarfs bravely jumped on the creature as it passed by them.

"Tie it up!" yelled Grumpy.

"Yeah, don't let it get away!" cried Doc.

As the dwarfs struggled to hold the creature, its metal head fell off and hit the ground with a thump, and in its place was a head they recognized immediately—it was Dopey!

"Aw, fuss and fiddlesticks," grumbled Grumpy. "All that trouble fer nothin'!"

When the dwarfs finally calmed down and helped Dopey to his feet, they showered him with questions. "Did you see the creature? How big was it? Was it a dragon? Was it breathing fire? What *was* it doing?"

Dopey quickly gestured that the creature was *sleeping*!

"He says it's a monster!" Doc cried. "A-asleep in our beds!"

"Let's attack!" growled Grumpy. "While it's still sleeping!"

Doc agreed. "Hurry, men," he shouted. "It's now or never!"

So the dwarfs marched bravely back into the house, this time determined to face whatever danger there was. They crept

quietly into the bedroom and right up to the beds where Snow White lay sleeping peacefully under the sheets.

They surrounded the beds, holding up picks and clubs as weapons. Doc slowly and shakily pulled back the covers.

The dwarfs were just about to strike when they saw Snow White. As one, they lowered their weapons and stood motionless.

Doc was the first to recover.

"Well . . . ah . . . ah," he stammered.

"What is it?" asked Happy, gazing at the sleeping princess.

"Why, I, it—it's," stuttered Doc, "it's a girl!"

Sneezy and Bashful both smiled.

"She's mighty purty," said Sneezy.

"She's *beautiful,*" said Bashful, blushing. "Just like an angel."

All the dwarfs were captivated by Snow White. All but Grumpy, that is. "Angel, huh!" he said sourly. "She's a female. And all females is poison. They're fulla wicked wiles."

"What're wicked wiles?" asked Bashful.

"I dunno," answered Grumpy. "But I'm against them!"

Doc told Grumpy not to speak so loudly or the lovely young girl might wake up.

"Aw, let her wake up," replied Grumpy. "She don't belong here nohow."

At that, Snow White's eyelids fluttered.

"She's waking up!" whispered Happy.

The dwarfs quickly hid at the foot of the beds.

Snow White yawned and opened her eyes. She sat up and looked around, remembering where she was.

"Oh dear," she said to herself. "I wonder if the children are—"

Just then she saw the dwarfs peeking over the edge of the bed boards.

"Oh!" cried Snow White as she pulled the covers up around her. But then she sat up straighter and stared in surprise.

"Why, you're not children at all," she said. "You're little men!"

Snow White smiled prettily and said, "How do you do."

"How do you do what?" answered Grumpy with a frown.

But Snow White was not ruffled by Grumpy's rudeness, and she just continued gaily, "Oh, you can talk. I'm so glad."

Snow White looked from one dwarf to the other and smiled. "Let me try to guess your names," she said, pointing first at Doc.

"You must be Doc."

"Yes," answered Doc politely.

Then she pointed at Sleepy, who was busy yawning.

"I *know* you're Sleepy," Snow White said.

Sleepy answered with a bob of his head.

Snow White looked at Dopey, who was gazing at her with large blue eyes.

"You must be Dopey," she said.

Dopey nodded excitedly.

She cocked her head and looked at Happy, who was smiling from ear to ear.

"And you've got to be Happy," Snow White said.

Happy chuckled in glee. "Why, that's right!" he cried. "How did you guess?"

Then she leaned forward to look at Bashful, who was trying to hide behind the others.

"You're Bashful," she said.

"Uh, yup. I mean—*gulp!*" Bashful answered, his face turning a bright pink.

Just then Sneezy piped up. "Can you guess—*a-a-chooo!*—who I am?"

Snow White giggled. "I would say you were Sneezy!" she answered.

Sneezy held a finger under his nose and said in a muffled voice, "Tha-tha-that's right. *A-choooo!*"

When Snow White finally came to Grumpy, she looked at his folded arms and stern expression and took the same pose.

"And you must be Grumpy," she said in a deep voice.

But Grumpy just turned to Doc and said, "*We* know who we are. Ask her who *she* is and what she's doing in our house!"

And so the dwarfs asked. Snow White told them who she was and all about her terrible flight through the forest.

When the dwarfs learned that she was the princess Snow White, they were honored to have her as a guest in their tiny forest home. All except Grumpy. He insisted that she should be made to leave.

Snow White looked at the dwarfs entreatingly.

"Please don't send me away," she pleaded. "If you do, she'll kill me!"

"Who?" they asked.

And so Snow White told the dwarfs all about her evil stepmother, the queen.

When she was finished, the dwarfs all clucked their tongues in sympathy.

"She's wicked," said Bashful.

"She's bad," said Happy.

"She's an old *witch*!" said Grumpy. "And I'm warning ya, if the queen finds Snow White here, she'll sweep down and wreak her vengeance on all of us!"

"But she doesn't know where I am," said Snow White.

"She doesn't? Heh!" answered Grumpy. "She knows everything!

"She's full of black magic," he continued. "She can make herself invisible. Why, she might even be in this room right now."

The other dwarfs looked around the room uneasily. But Snow White sat up straighter.

"Oh, she'll never find me here," she said brightly. "And if you let me stay, I can help with the chores. I'm a good cook, too."

"A good cook!" cried the dwarfs, suddenly remembering their own hunger and the aroma coming from the kettle.

"She stays!" shouted the dwarfs in spite of Grumpy's glowering face.

CHAPTER SIX

now White went downstairs, followed by seven hungry dwarfs. She went over to the kettle, dipped a spoon in, and tasted the contents. The dwarfs sniffed the air.

"It's soup—hooray!" they cried as they made a rush for the dining table.

Snow White put up her hand.

"Just a minute," she said. "Supper's not quite ready. You'll just have time to wash."

"Wash!" cried Doc.

"Wash?" said Bashful.

"Wash!" yelped Happy.

Grumpy threw down the spoon he had just picked up.

"Heh, I know'd there be a catch to it!" he said.

"Why wash?" said Bashful. "We ain't going nowhere."

"Yeah," Doc chimed in. "And 'tain't New Year's or anything."

Snow White put her hands on her hips and raised her eyebrows. She looked at the dwarfs.

"Oh, perhaps you have washed already," she said with a knowing smile. "Recently?"

Doc nodded and said, "Yes, that's right. Perhaps we, er, yes, perhaps we have."

"When?" asked Snow White.

"Er, like you said, er, recently," answered Doc.

The other dwarfs murmured happily in agreement.

"Ohhhh," said Snow White with a suspicious look. "*Recently*. Then let me see your hands," she said in a firm voice.

The dwarfs lined up and, one by one, hesitantly showed Snow White their hands. Each pair was dirtier than the last.

"Oh, how shocking!" said Snow White. "Worse than I thought."

She shook her head slowly from side to side.

"I don't think that will do," she said to the shamefaced men.

Then she pointed at the door.

"March straight outside and wash, or you'll not get a bite to eat," she said with conviction.

The dwarfs turned and slowly walked out of the house, moaning and groaning to themselves. All except Grumpy. He stood with his arms folded and a sour expression on his face.

"Well, what about you?" asked Snow White. "Aren't you going to wash?"

Instead of answering, Grumpy just sulked.

"What's the matter?" said Snow White teasingly. "Cat got your tongue?"

At that, Grumpy stuck out his tongue and headed out of the house in a huff.

The other dwarfs were gathered around the big wooden tub in the yard.

"Courage, men, courage," Doc urged.

"But the water's wet!" moaned Happy.

"Cold, too!" complained Sneezy. "We ain't gonna *really* do it, are we?"

"Well, er," said Doc, struggling for a good reason. "It'll please the princess."

Happy beamed at that.

"Okay, then," he said, looking at the water doubtfully. "I'll take a chance for her."

"Me, too," agreed the rest all together.

Grumpy sat on a barrel close by, listening to the others.

"You see?" he said. "Her wiles are beginnin' to work."

Then he pointed at the dwarfs and lectured.

"I'm a-warning ya. Ya give 'em an inch and they'll walk all over ya!"

Doc looked sternly at Grumpy and told the other dwarfs not to listen to him. And with that, the men bravely started to scrub their faces, wash their hands, brush their teeth, and comb their hair.

When they were through, they looked at each other in awe. They hardly recognized themselves.

"Hah," cried Grumpy, still sitting on the barrel. "Bunch of old nanny goats. Ya make me sick! Next thing ya know, she'll be tyin' your beards up in pink ribbons and smellin' ya up with that stuff called, er, perfumy. Hah! What a fine bunch of water lilies!"

The dwarfs looked at Grumpy and then at each other. Then they all nodded.

"Get 'im!" Doc suddenly cried.

The dwarfs pounced on Grumpy and carried him over to the tub.

"Hey, lemme loose, ya fools!" Grumpy yelled as he squirmed to free himself.

But the dwarfs paid no attention. Instead they dumped Grumpy right into the tub of soapy water and started to scrub him good.

"Now scrub hard, men!" Doc urged. "It can't be denied, he'll look mighty cute as soon as he's dried."

Grumpy fumed and fussed.

"You'll pay for this!" he cried as he continued to struggle to get out of the tub. Suddenly they heard a loud clang as Snow White banged a spoon on the kettle.

"Supper!" she called out.

"Supper!" the men shouted.

They all let go of Grumpy at once, and he dropped back into the tub, sputtering and blowing bubbles as he gulped a mouthful of soapsuds.

Muttering and complaining, Grumpy finally got out of the tub and headed for the house. With a "Hmph!" he joined the other dwarfs now seated at the table, eagerly awaiting their supper.

CHAPTER SEVEN

ack at the castle, the queen was once again consulting her magic mirror. But as she waited calmly for the expected reply, it said instead,

Over the seven jeweled hills,
Beyond the seventh fall,
In the cottage of the seven dwarfs
Dwells Snow White,
Fairest one of all.

Shocked and outraged, the evil queen realized that she had been tricked. Snow White was still alive! The huntsman had not brought back Snow White's heart in the box but that of a forest animal!

The queen immediately began to plot a way to put an end to Snow White on her own.

"I'll go to the dwarfs' cottage myself," she muttered, "in a disguise so complete, no one will ever suspect it's me."

She swept down a flight of stone steps into her deep, dark dungeon. As the queen made her way across the dingy chamber, scurrying rats squealed and ran for cover. Spiders, beetles, and a host of other crawling things crept away at the sight of the evil queen. The only creature that didn't move was the queen's pet raven, who watched her approach with unblinking eyes and an evil expression to match her own.

But the queen took no notice of these things. She went straight to her book of black magic and flipped through its pages until she found what she wanted.

"Ah," she murmured. "A peddler's disguise. Perfect!"

She went over to a table cluttered with vials and beakers filled with all sorts of bubbling, smoking liquids. She selected one beaker and poured a steaming green liquid into a large goblet.

"First, some mummy dust to make me old," she said as she sprinkled a fine gray powder into the glass. "To shroud my clothes, the black of night." She added a drop of black liquid. "To age my voice, a drop of crow's blood." Then a ruby red drop was added to the brew.

The queen continued mixing her potion until she was satisfied that she had done everything exactly right. When she was finished, she held the goblet before her. The brew bubbled and hissed and spilled over the rim of the glass. She smiled grimly, and then with one quick motion she swallowed the foul liquid.

As soon as she had done so, the queen clutched her throat as if she were choking. The dungeon seemed to spin crazily around her, and a powerful wind sprang up, rustling her robes and hair as if she were in the midst of a hurricane.

The queen moaned as she shook violently and then crum-

pled over as if a powerful hand were squeezing the youth from her body.

And as she quivered in the grips of the magic potion, her lustrous black hair began turning a dingy white, and her smooth face started to fold into hideous wrinkles. Her long beautiful fingers twisted into clawlike talons, and her elegant robe changed color and shape until it was no more than a faded black rag.

Suddenly a flash of brilliant green light filled the dungeon, and when it was gone, a haggard old witch stood in place of the once-beautiful queen! She shrieked in both triumph and agony as the awful transformation reached its final stage.

The witch glanced in a mirror and cackled.

"Yes, a perfect disguise," she croaked, and hobbled over to her book of spells once more.

"And now," she hissed, "I must plan a special sort of death for one so fair. What shall it be?"

The queen flipped through the pages until she stopped and cried, "Ah, yes! Perfect. A poisoned apple!"

She read the spell aloud as her gnarled fingers traced the words.

"One taste of the poisoned apple and the victim's eyes will close forever in the sleeping death."

The old hag threw back her head and laughed long and loud, the sound echoing throughout the deep, dark dungeon like the shrieks of a hundred black crows.

CHAPTER EIGHT

s darkness settled over the forest, music rang out from inside the dwarfs' cottage while they entertained their new guest. Doc played the bass; Happy, Dopey, and Sneezy yodeled and danced; Sleepy played the horn, lazily keeping time with his foot; and Bashful played the accordion and sang. Even Grumpy grudgingly joined in. He played the organ and yodeled in a low, growling voice. Snow White danced and sang along with them all.

When the song was over, Snow White sank into a chair and sighed contentedly.

"That was fun!" she said, her face flushed with color. "You were all so marvelous."

"Now you do somethin'," said Happy.

"Well, what shall I do?" asked Snow White.

"Tell us a story," piped up Sleepy.

All the dwarfs nodded in agreement.

"Yes, tell us a story," they cried.

"A *true* story," added Happy.

"A looove story," said Bashful with a blush.

Snow White looked at their eager faces and gathered them around her.

"Well," she began. "Once there was a princess—"

"Was the princess you?" Doc interrupted.

Snow White nodded gently as she continued.

"And she fell in love with a prince," she said.

"Was it—*a-chooo!*—hard to do?" asked Sneezy.

Snow White shook her head and laughed.

"It wasn't hard at all. It was very easy. Anyone could see that the prince was as good as he was charming."

Then Snow White looked away for a moment and sighed. "I knew he was the only one for me."

The dwarfs showered her with questions.

"Was he big and tall?"

"Did he say he loved ya?"

"Did he steal a kiss?"

"No, but he *was* romantic," answered Snow White. "I couldn't help being drawn to him. I had always known that someday I would meet someone I could love, and I did."

Then Snow White smiled and started to sing in a soft, pleasant voice. And through the song, she poured out all the secret longings of her young heart.

Just as the song was ending, the clock struck the hour.

"Oh my goodness," cried Snow White. "It's past bedtime. Go right upstairs, all of you," Snow White said, playfully shooing the dwarfs out of the room.

"Hold on there, men," Doc cried. "The princess will sleep upstairs in our beds."

"But where will you sleep?" asked Snow White.

"Why, er," answered Doc, "we'll be as bug as a snug in a rug—I mean, as snug as a bug in a rug down here."

"In a pig's eye," snapped Grumpy.

"Yep, in a pigsty—I mean, a pig's eye," echoed Doc. Then he realized he had agreed with Grumpy's sour remark, and he shook his head in dismay.

"We'll be comfortable, won't we, men?" he said to the dwarfs, looking especially at Grumpy.

"Oh yes," they answered, not sure whether they meant it or not.

Doc turned back to Snow White and said, "Go right up now, uh, my dear."

"Well, if you insist," answered Snow White.

Then she smiled sweetly at them and said good night.

Snow White knelt beside the beds and murmured low, "Bless the seven little men who have been so kind to me, and . . . and may my dreams come true."

She started to rise, but quickly knelt down again.

"Oh yes," she added. "And please make Grumpy like me."

And with that, she crept into the beds and pulled up the covers.

CHAPTER NINE

oon the whole house was still, with only the snoring of the seven dwarfs downstairs to break the silence. Outside, the forest, too, was quiet, its creatures having settled down for the night.

But there was someone who was wide awake and busily concocting a deadly present—the evil queen!

The old hag held a large apple on a string over a steaming cauldron.

"Dip the apple in the brew," the queen-witch intoned. "Let the sleeping death seep through."

The apple disappeared into the bubbling liquid, and when the witch pulled it out again a few seconds later, the brew dripped down the apple's sides, leaving the shape of a skull on its skin.

"Ah," sighed the witch. "On the skin, the symbol of what lies within. Now turn red," she commanded, "to tempt Snow White, to make her hunger for a bite."

At that, the apple turned a beautiful ruby red.

The witch held the apple in her hand and thrust it at her pet raven.

"Have a bite?" she murmured wickedly.

The bird shuddered and backed away from the poisoned treat.

The witch laughed in mischievous glee.

"It's not for you, anyway," she cried in a raspy voice. "It's for Snow White! When she breaks the tender peel to taste the apple in my hand," the hag went on, "her breath will still, her blood congeal. Then I'll be fairest in the land!"

Then the witch paused and frowned.

"Wait," she said to the raven. "There may be an antidote. Nothing must be overlooked."

She scurried over to her book of spells and flipped through it once again. Suddenly her bony fingers stopped at one of the pages.

"Ah, I was right. Here it is," she said.

The witch started to read.

"The victim of the sleeping death can be revived only by love's first kiss.

"Love's first kiss!" she hissed. "Bah, no fear of *that*. The dwarfs will think she's dead, and they'll bury her *alive*!

"Buried alive!" she screeched over and over as she grabbed a basketful of other apples and gently placed the poisoned one among them.

With the basket of apples under one arm, the witch left the dungeon and descended the stone steps leading to the river that streamed beneath the castle. She got into a small boat and started to row away into the night. A pale moon hung overhead, and shadows fell over her craggy features, making her face look like a ghastly white skull.

CHAPTER TEN

he next morning, Snow White rose to see a bright yellow sun and blue sky peeking through the branches of the trees overhead.

She had just enough time to give the men a hearty breakfast before they went off to work in the mine.

As the dwarfs were leaving, Doc said, "Now, don't forgit, my dear. The old queen's a fly—er, I mean, a sly one."

He wagged a finger at the princess.

"She's fulla witchcraft," he continued. "So beware of strangers."

"Don't worry," answered Snow White. "I'll be all right."

One by one she kissed the dwarfs on the forehead and said good-bye. And one by one they warned her to be alert. Grumpy was the last to leave, and just before he joined the others, he cleared his throat and said, "Now, I'm warnin' ya. Don't let nobody or nothin' in the house."

Snow White looked down at him and smiled.

"Oh, Grumpy, you *do* like me after all!" she cried.

And with that, she bent down and planted a kiss on his forehead.

"Hey, stop that mushy stuff," scowled Grumpy as he broke away from Snow White's hug and stomped off. But after a few steps, he turned around and gazed at Snow White with an adoring expression. Snow White blew him a kiss. Grumpy held his smile for a few seconds more until he suddenly realized what he was doing. He immediately scowled again and hurried off to join the others.

Not far from the cottage, the wicked witch was making her way through the forest.

"The little men will be off," she cackled to herself. "And she'll be alone. Alone, with a harmless old peddler woman!" She laughed long and loud, and two vultures in a nearby tree flapped away in alarm. But she quickly grew silent as she saw the cottage of the seven dwarfs come into view.

CHAPTER ELEVEN

s soon as the dwarfs had left, Snow White busied herself preparing food for that evening. She felt it was the least she could do to repay the dwarfs for their kindness.

After cutting up some carrots and potatoes, Snow White decided to bake some gooseberry pies for dessert. She was near the window and just putting the finishing touches on one of them when a dark shadow passed over her cutting board.

Snow White looked up in surprise and saw an old woman peering into the house from the window.

"All alone, my pet?" asked the old woman.

"Why . . . why, yes, I am, but . . . ," answered Snow White, a little frightened of the strange woman.

"The little men are not here?" cut in the old woman.

"No, they're not," said Snow White.

The old woman smiled.

"Hmmm," she said. "Makin' pies?"

"Yes, gooseberry pies," answered Snow White, more at ease. After all, this was only a harmless peddler woman.

The old woman smiled toothlessly.

"It's apple pies that make menfolk's mouths water," she said.

Then she took the deep red apple from her basket and held it up. "Pies made from apples like these," said the old woman.

"Oh, they do look delicious," said Snow White.

"Yes," murmured the old peddler, "but wait until you taste one, dearie."

Then she held the poisoned apple out to Snow White.

"Like to try one, hmmm?" the old woman asked.

Snow White stepped back from the window a bit, not sure of what to do. Her animal friends fretted and paced anxiously in the woods nearby. The birds had twittered in alarm at the sight of the old peddler, and now they flapped their wings in helpless frustration as they watched Snow White about to take the tempting treat.

But just as Snow White reached for the apple, the birds swooped down and knocked it from the old woman's hand. Then they fluttered around her, pecking at her head and body.

The witch waved her feeble arms around and cried, "Oh, go away! Leave me alone!"

Snow White ran out of the house and shooed the birds away.

"Stop it. Stop it right now," Snow White cried.

The birds flew off back into the trees, where they perched restlessly.

"Shame on you," Snow White scolded. "Frightening a poor old lady."

The birds hung their heads, not knowing what to do.

Snow White went to the old woman, who by now was on her hands and knees recovering the apple.

The princess helped the woman to her feet, then said, "I'm sorry, I don't know what has gotten into those birds. They are usually so gentle and kind."

The old woman nodded absently, then grasped her chest and cried convincingly, "Oh, my poor heart."

Snow White held the woman up by the arm and looked at her with concern.

"Please take me into the house," the woman said. "Let me rest a while. Perhaps I may have a glass of water?"

Snow White nodded and took the old peddler into the house.

The birds and other animals rushed to the window to peek inside. They watched as Snow White helped the peddler into a chair and then gave her a cup of water. When Snow White turned away a moment, the old woman leered at them. The animals backed away and, one by one, scampered off to find the seven dwarfs.

CHAPTER TWELVE

he animals crashed through thicket and brush as if a fire were chasing them. Finally, they reached the mine and started to push and prod the dwarfs in the direction of the cottage. The men thought the animals had gone mad.

"What ails these crazy critters?" cried Doc.

"They've gone plumb daffy!" yelled Bashful.

"Go on, git!" cried Doc as a deer bumped him from behind.

Then he turned to the other dwarfs.

"These pesky critters won't stop," he said.

" 'Tain't natural," cried Happy, flapping his arms to shoo away the birds.

"There's somethin'—*a-choo!*—wrong," cried Sneezy.

Even Grumpy agreed. "They ain't actin' this way for nothin'," he grumbled.

Sleepy looked at everyone with half-closed eyes.

"Maybe the old queen's got Snow White," he said as he stifled a yawn.

"*The queen!*" cried Doc.

"*Snow White!*" cried the others.

Grumpy pounded his fist into his hand.

"The queen'll kill her! We've gotta save her!" he cried.

Then he hopped onto the back of a deer and said, "Giddyap!"

One by one the dwarfs leapt onto deer and galloped back toward their cottage.

The strange parade of running creatures hurtled through the forest, leaping over rocks and streams.

"Faster!" Doc urged the others. "We haven't got a moment to lose!"

Meanwhile, back at the cottage, the witch had pretended to recover her strength and was now carrying on a warm conversation with Snow White.

She held up the poisoned apple once more.

"Because you've been so good to old granny," she said, "I'll share a secret with you."

Snow White leaned forward in interest.

"This is no ordinary apple," the old woman said as she got to her feet. "It's a magic *wishing* apple!"

"A wishing apple?" said Snow White.

"Yes," answered the witch. "One bite and all your dreams will come true."

"Really?" said Snow White.

"Yes, girlie," murmured the peddler. "Now make a wish and take a bite."

With a crooked smile, she held out the poisoned apple to Snow White.

CHAPTER THIRTEEN

The dwarfs raced on through the forest, hoping to reach home and find Snow White safe. But time was running out.

"There must be something your little heart desires," murmured the woman, still holding the apple in her hand. "Perhaps there is someone you love?"

"Well, there is someone," answered Snow White slowly.

"I thought so," answered the woman slyly. "Ha, ha, old granny knows a young girl's heart."

The old woman handed the apple to Snow White and patted her hand. "Now take the apple, dearie, and make a wish," she said.

Snow White gazed at the apple and said, "I wish . . ."

"That's it. Go on, go on," the witch urged.

". . . that I will meet my prince again, and together we will travel to his kingdom," Snow White said more boldly.

"Fine," smiled the old woman. "Now take a bite—hurry! Don't let the wish grow cold."

Snow White held the ruby red apple up and took a bite. As soon as she had done so, she tottered on her feet.

"Oh, I feel so strange!" she cried.

The old woman rubbed her hands in satisfaction as she intoned, "Her breath will still."

"Oh," cried Snow White as she put her hand to her forehead.

"Her blood congeal," hissed the old woman.

"Oh," moaned Snow White one final time before she sank to the ground and lay as still as death. The apple fell out of her hand and rolled away.

The old woman dropped all pretense now and threw back her head and howled.

"It is done!" she cried. "Now I'll be fairest in the land!"

The witch turned and hurried out of the cottage and into the woods. A sudden crack of lightning ripped across the sky, followed by a torrent of rain. It was as if the heavens themselves were angry at the witch for her wicked deed. But the old hag wasn't afraid. She had finally gotten rid of Snow White and could feel only joy at her achievement.

She cackled low in her throat as she hobbled through the woods, anxious to return to her castle and her former self. She started to climb toward a small cliff when she saw the seven dwarfs coming straight at her.

"There she goes!" cried Grumpy. "After her!"

The dwarfs chased the witch as she scrambled up the rocky hill.

The old woman cried out in frustration as she saw the dwarfs in close pursuit. Now frightened and desperate, she climbed farther out onto a long slab of rock overhanging a deep ravine. The wind and rain lashed at her face and clothing.

The witch looked wildly around her as she realized she was cornered.

"I'm trapped," she cried. "What will I do? The meddling little fools."

Then she picked up a broken tree limb from the ground, and using it as a lever, she started to pry loose a huge boulder that was perched on the slab. Her magic now gave her the strength of ten men, and the boulder started to teeter back and forth.

"I'll fix you! I'll fix you!" she cried out to the dwarfs. "I'll crush your bones!"

"Look out!" cried Grumpy. "She's going to roll that boulder right over us!"

The witch laughed triumphantly as the boulder started to come loose. But just as it was about to roll down onto the dwarfs, a bolt of lightning struck the outcropping rock. In an instant, it shattered and fell away, carrying the witch and the boulder with it.

The witch gave out a long, horrifying shriek as she fell all the way to the jagged rocks below.

One by one the dwarfs approached the edge of the broken slab and looked down. They couldn't see the witch, but when they saw two vultures swoop down with greedy eyes, they knew she was gone forever.

When they finally reached their cottage, they found Snow White laying motionless on the floor.

"She . . . she's dead," cried Sleepy.

The others nodded sadly. The queen had won after all.

CHAPTER FOURTEEN

he dwarfs could not bear to bury the princess, so they fashioned a coffin of gold and glass and placed Snow White in it. Then they carried the coffin to a peaceful glen in the woods. Every day, the dwarfs kept vigil at the coffin and placed flowers around it.

One day the following spring, the dwarfs were keeping their usual vigil. They had opened the glass top and placed a bouquet of flowers in Snow White's hands. Then they knelt before the coffin and bowed their heads.

They were surprised to see a handsome prince ride into the clearing on a white horse. He was the very same young man who had first met Snow White at the well. He had heard of the beautiful maiden who slept in the glass coffin and was curious to see if it was the same princess he had once met.

As he approached the coffin, the prince realized that it *was* the same girl. Sadly, he knelt by the coffin and bowed his head. Then he bent over the still form and gave Snow White one farewell kiss. And when he did, he saw to his surprise and joy that Snow White's eyes fluttered open.

She was alive!

Snow White slowly sat up and smiled. It was as if she had just woken up from a good night's sleep. When she saw the prince, her eyes lit up in surprise, and she held out her arms to him. The prince quickly took her in his arms and lifted her up.

For a moment the dwarfs stood silent and unbelieving. But they soon threw their hats in the air and yelled and cheered in delight.

When they had finally calmed down again, Snow White went over and looked at each one of them fondly.

"You have been good, kind friends," she said in a soft voice. "And I shall never forget you."

One by one the dwarfs stood by while Snow White kissed each of them on the forehead.

"Good-bye, Princess," they called as the prince lifted Snow White onto his horse.

"Good-bye," she called back.

Then the prince took the reins of his steed and slowly led it away.

"Good-bye!" Snow White called out once more as she and the prince slowly disappeared from view.

When Snow White and the prince had gone, the dwarfs looked at each other and smiled. Even though they would miss her, they knew Snow White's wish had finally come true. She had found her true love, and she would live happily ever after. And that made them happy, too. Even Grumpy.